This
Nature Storybook
*belongs to:*

_____

_____

_____

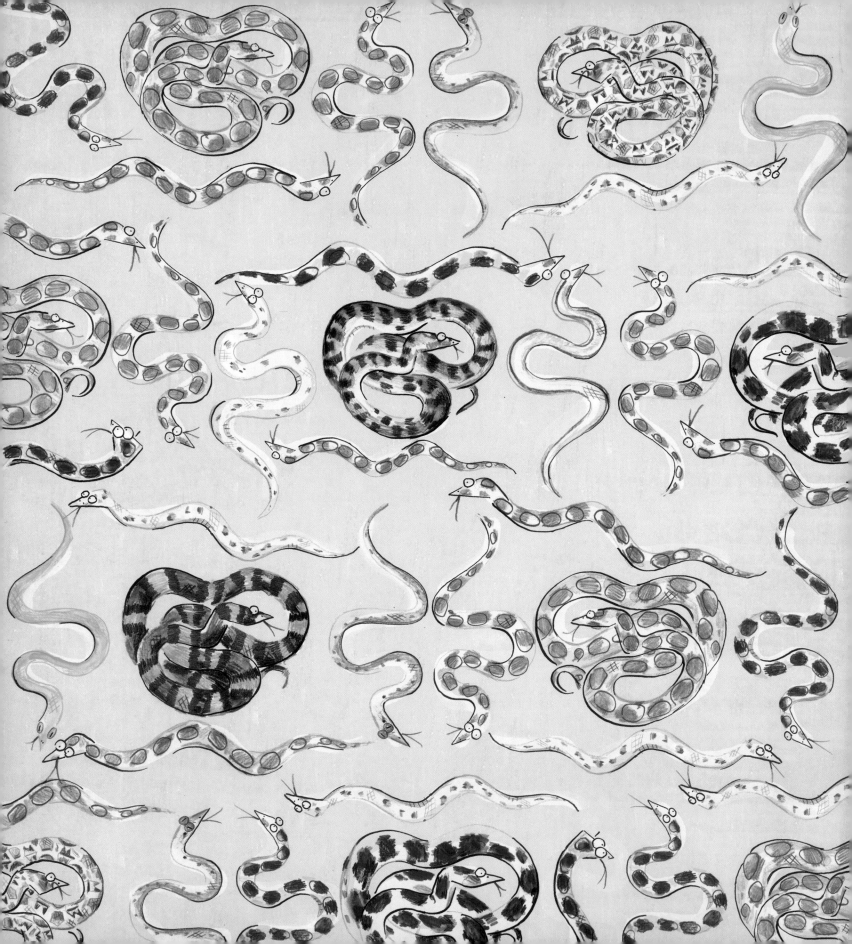

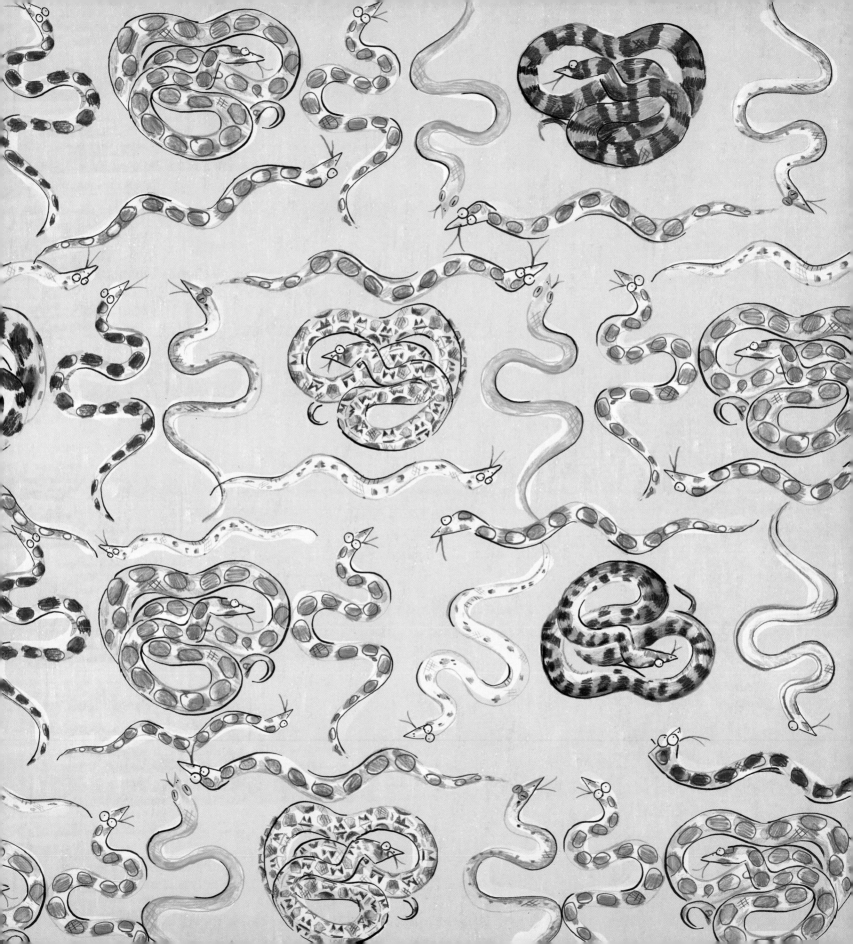

*For Toes and Gee, Poborsky and Solskjaer — the geckos, the corn snake round the light bulb and the rat snake under the floorboards  N. D.*

*For my nephew, Raul  L. L.*

First published 2015 by Walker Books Ltd
87 Vauxhall Walk, London SE11 5HJ

This edition published 2016

10 9 8 7 6 5 4 3 2 1

Text © 2015 Nicola Davies
Illustrations © 2015 Luciano Lozano

The right of Nicola Davies and Luciano Lozano to be identified as author and illustrator respectively of this work has been asserted by them in accordance with the Copyright, Designs and Patents Act 1988

This book has been typeset in Ashley Script and Vag Rounded

Printed in China

British Library Cataloguing in Publication Data: a catalogue record for this book is available from the British Library

ISBN 978-1-4063-6568-9

www.walker.co.uk

**WALKER BOOKS**
AND SUBSIDIARIES
LONDON • BOSTON • SYDNEY • AUCKLAND

# I ~~DON'T~~ LIKE SNAKES

**Nicola Davies**

Illustrated by
**Luciano Lozano**

Some families keep dogs, or cats, or birds.
But my family keeps **SNAKES**. They love them!

So when I said, "I really, **really**,
**REALLY** don't like snakes!"

they all said,

## "WHY?"

7

"Because," I said, "they slither!"

"Snakes HAVE to slither," said my mum. "They've got no legs, so they bend like an S and use their ribs and scales to grip. It's the only way they can move."

8

# Snakes slither in different ways

## Concertina slithering

The snake grips the ground at its tail end with the scales on its underside and stretches forward with its head end.
Then it grips at the head and pulls the tail end forward, and starts all over again.

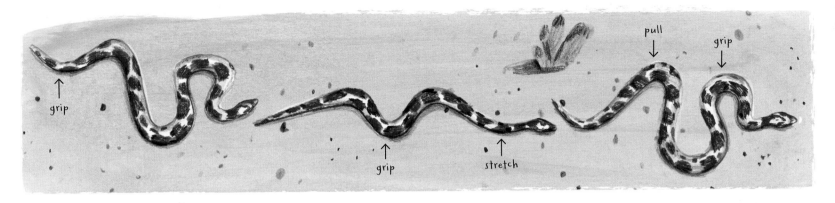

## Serpentine slithering

The snake uses its scales for grip and presses against the ground and objects
on either side with the curves of its body, to push itself forward.

## Caterpillar crawling

When a snake needs to move without any side-to-side wiggling, the scales under its head and neck grip the ground
while its tail end scrunches upward and forward, like a looping caterpillar.

"And look what snakes can do," said Dad. "They can sidewind over sand, twine through trees, swim, climb — even fly!"

"OK," I said. "That's pretty clever."

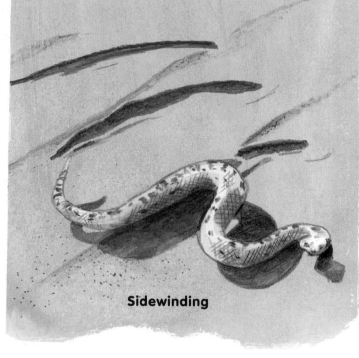

**Sidewinding**

On soft slipping sand, a snake moves by lifting its head and neck off the ground, gripping with just two points on its body and s-bending between them.

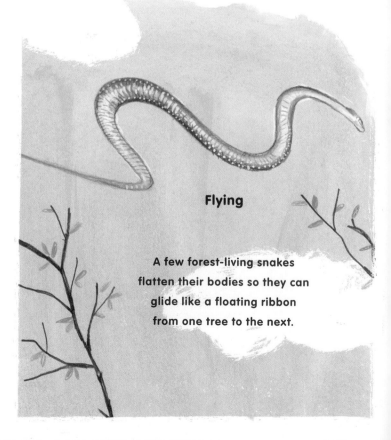

**Flying**

A few forest-living snakes flatten their bodies so they can glide like a floating ribbon from one tree to the next.

**Twining**

Snakes can twine around branches or
stretch their bodies across big gaps
to move through trees.

**Climbing**

Gripping with their belly scales and using caterpillar
crawling, snakes can climb tree trunks and walls.

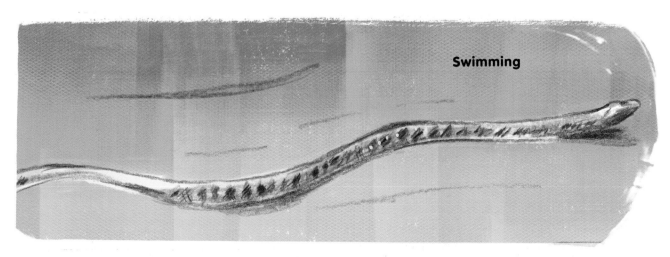

**Swimming**

Many kinds of
snake can
swim and some
live in rivers
and even
the sea.

"But what about their slimy,
scaly skin? It's icky!"

"Snakes aren't slimy," said Mum.
"If you touch their
skin it's dry. It looks
wet because they have a
shiny, see-through outer skin.

When that's worn out or
outgrown, like your old clothes
that get too scruffy or too small,
the snake just sheds it.
And there's new skin underneath."

12

**The snake wriggles out of its skin the way you pull your foot out of a sock, leaving the old skin inside out!**

snakes even shed the skin covering their eyes

Rattlesnakes keep bits of old skin on their tails to make a warning "rattle" sound when they wiggle them

13

"And as for snakes being scaly," said Dad, "their scales are like armour. They make mosaic _patterns_, so a snake can stand out like a warning ... or almost disappear!"

Corn Snake

Gaboon Viper

Coral Snake

"OK," I said, "that's pretty cool."

14

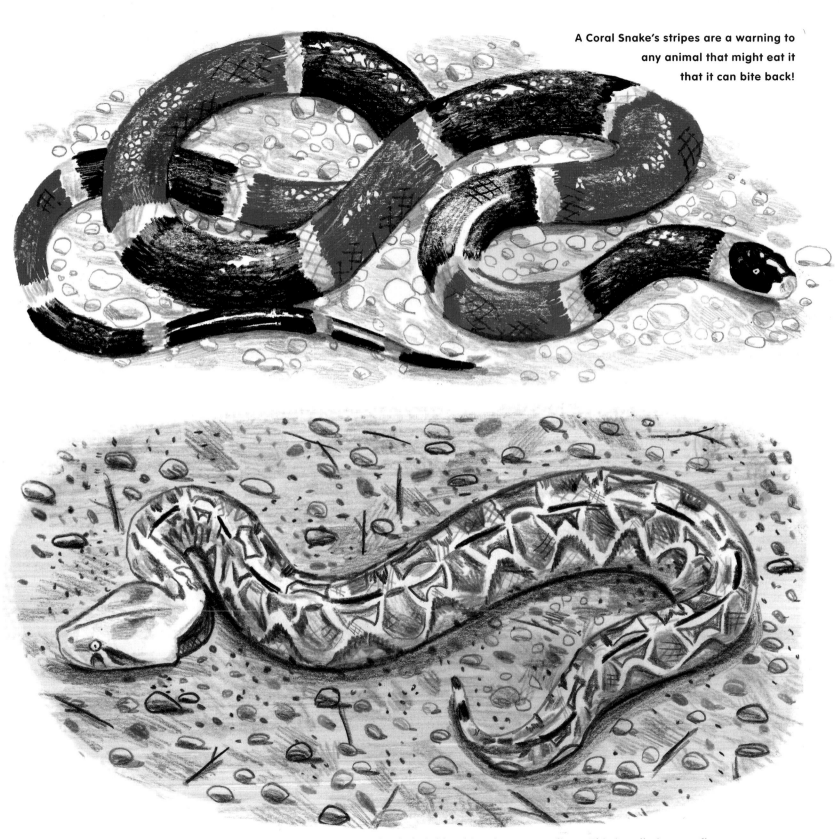

A Coral Snake's stripes are a warning to any animal that might eat it that it can bite back!

The colour and pattern of the Gaboon Viper's scales help it blend into its surroundings. This is called camouflage and it means snakes can hide from animals they want to eat – and ones that might eat them!

"But I still don't like their flicky tongues!"

"Snakes smell with their tongues," said Mum. "They flick them out to collect smells. All snakes are hunters and smelling is how they find their prey."

"OK," I said. "That IS interesting."

16

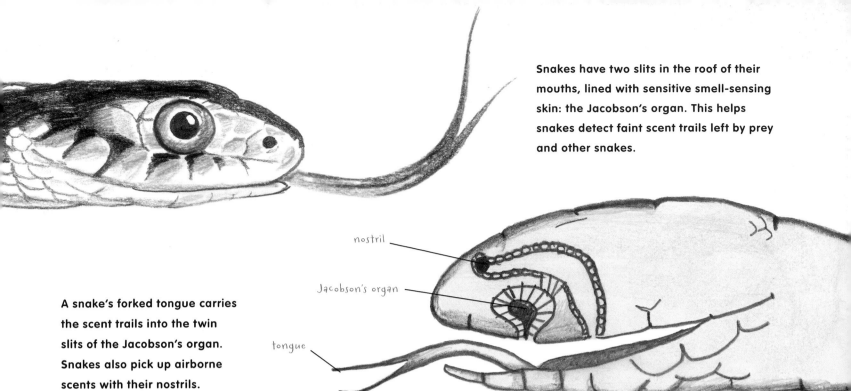

Snakes have two slits in the roof of their mouths, lined with sensitive smell-sensing skin: the Jacobson's organ. This helps snakes detect faint scent trails left by prey and other snakes.

nostril

Jacobson's organ

tongue

A snake's forked tongue carries the scent trails into the twin slits of the Jacobson's organ. Snakes also pick up airborne scents with their nostrils.

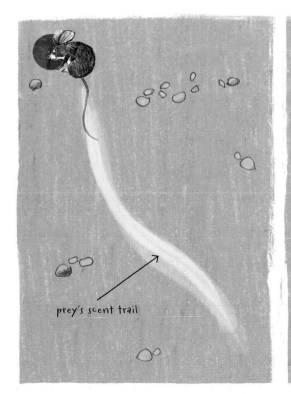

prey's scent trail

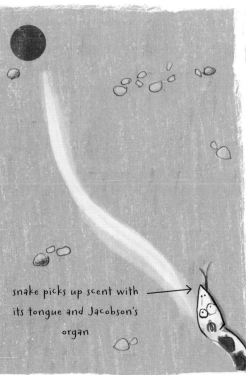

snake picks up scent with its tongue and Jacobson's organ

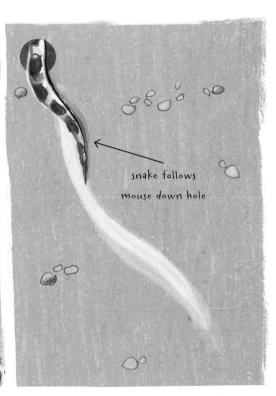

snake follows mouse down hole

"But I STILL don't like the way they stare! It's creepy."

"They stare," said Dad, "because they can't blink. Snakes don't have eyelids! But looking at their eyes can tell you how they do their hunting."

18

Night-time hunters tend to have slit-shaped pupils. Horizontal slits help snakes that chase prey, like the Vine Snake. Vertical slits are better for ambush hunters, like the Children's Python.

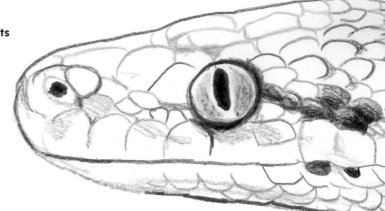

Children's Python

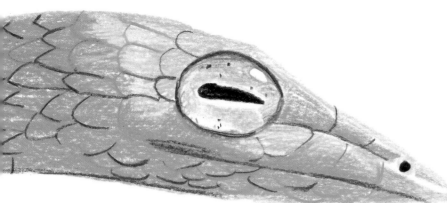

Vine Snake

Daytime hunters that chase prey, like the fast-moving Boomslang, have rounded pupils. The pupils of other daytime hunters, like the Slug-eating Snake, can close to a pinprick to protect sensitive eyes from bright daylight.

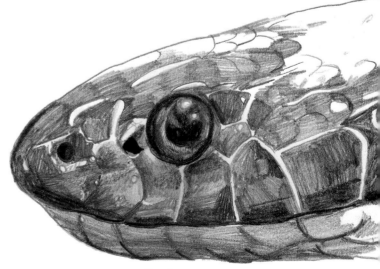

Slug-eating Snake

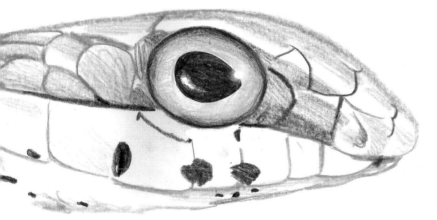

Boomslang

Some snakes, like the Pit Viper, hunt when it's too dark for even the best eyes to see. They have heat-sensitive pits below their eyes so they can feel their prey's body heat.

Pit Viper

"OK," I said. "Maybe now I know something about them, I do like snakes — just a little bit!"

"You do?" said my brother. "Well in that case, I'll tell you something that'll really scare you — how they kill things.

Some snakes use **POISON**. They have hollow fangs, like a doctor's needle, which inject venom. They strike like lightning, killing with just one bite. Their dinner dies in moments.

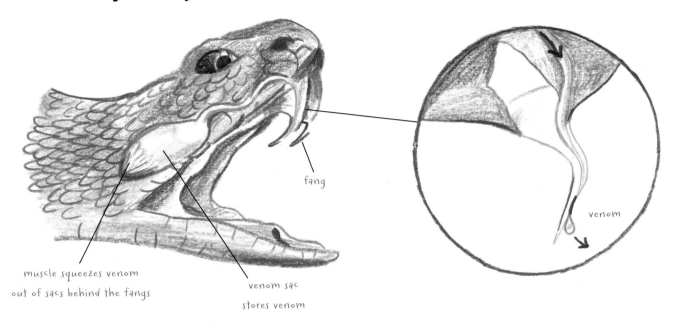

muscle squeezes venom
out of sacs behind the fangs

venom sac
stores venom

fang

venom

Some snakes have a bite so venomous it can kill a human in minutes.
Only people trained as snake-handlers should go near any venomous snake.

Fangs can inject venom with
the smallest pinprick.

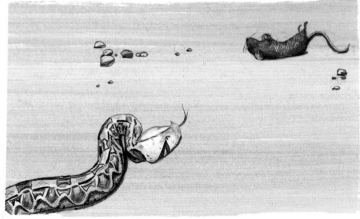

Venom kills fast, so even if the prey runs away it doesn't
get far and the snake can track it by smell.

Other snakes are **STRANGLERS** – they use their body like
a rope to tie prey up and squeeze the life out of it.

Snakes that kill like
this are called constrictors.
They wrap their bodies round their
prey and squeeze tight until they feel
its heart stop beating. Most snakes are shorter than
a skipping rope and eat mice and rats, but some are big
enough to kill animals as large as a deer or kangaroo.

But however snakes kill their prey, there's only one way
they can eat it. They don't have claws to rip it to bits

22

or the right kind of teeth for chewing, so they have to swallow it whole! So," my brother said, "how d'you like that?"

"I like it just fine!" I said. "What's more, I've got something to tell YOU...

It's something I've found out for **MYSELF** ... and that's how snakes have their babies.

Some snakes give birth to live babies. But most lay eggs with leathery shells that can take months to hatch.

Live snakes are born inside a see-through sac that they wriggle out of immediately – and they may stay near Mum for only a few hours.

A few snake mums wrap their bodies round their eggs to guard them. But most just leave them hidden somewhere safe. As long as they are warm and moist, the baby snakes inside will grow.

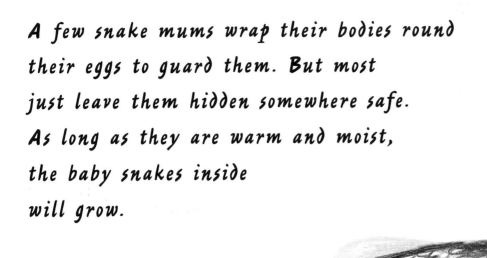

When they're ready, they wriggle out of their eggs and then they're off into the world...

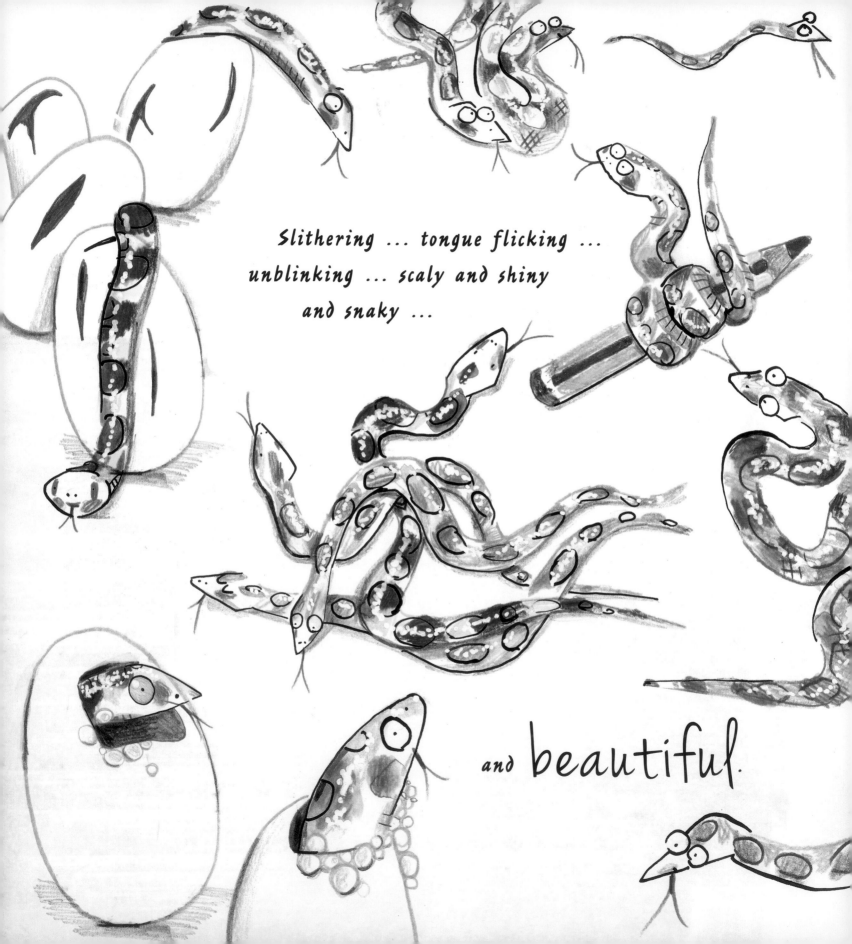

Slithering ... tongue flicking ...
unblinking ... scaly and shiny
and snaky ...

and beautiful.

And do you know what?" I said, "I really really
REEEEEALLLLY LIKE THEM!"

# ALL ABOUT SNAKES

There are almost **3,000** different species (kinds) of snake in the world. They are found everywhere except for the Arctic and Antarctic, New Zealand, Ireland and remote islands in the ocean. Some are as small as a shoelace and some big enough to swallow a child. They thrive in almost every kind of habitat and can even be found living in the sea. Their beauty and variety demonstrate the amazing things that can be done with a body that is really just a tube!

Threadsnake
10 cm (4 in)

Green Anaconda
6.6 m (22 ft)

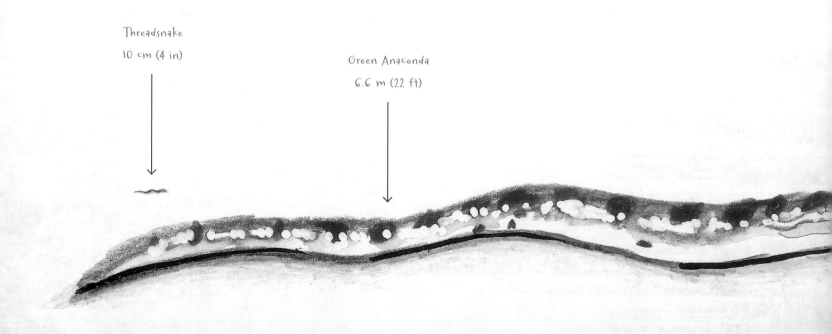

## INDEX

Look up the pages to find out about all these snake things. Don't forget to look at both kinds of word – *this kind* and this kind.

## ABOUT THE AUTHOR

Nicola Davies trained as a zoologist with a special interest in marine mammals, but she also loves reptiles – especially snakes. She wasn't allowed to keep a snake as a child, but later on she enjoyed sharing her daughter's Corn Snake and Rat Snake. She's encountered snakes on her travels around the world – most recently a huge Cottonmouth in a creek in Louisiana, USA, which was a big surprise for both Nicola and the snake.

## ABOUT THE ILLUSTRATOR

Luciano Lozano lives in Barcelona and his illustrations are published regularly in magazines and books. Of *I (Don't) Like Snakes* he says, "I've loved drawing this family and their pet snakes. I drew until they made me smile and, sometimes, they even smiled back. I hope they smile at you too."

## BIBLIOGRAPHY

*The New Encyclopedia of Snakes* by Chris Mattison
Princeton University Press (2007)

*The New Encyclopedia of Reptiles and Amphibians*
edited by Tim Halliday and Kraig Adler
Oxford University Press (2002)

*Snakes: The Evolution of Mystery In Nature*
by Harry W. Greene
University of California Press (2000)

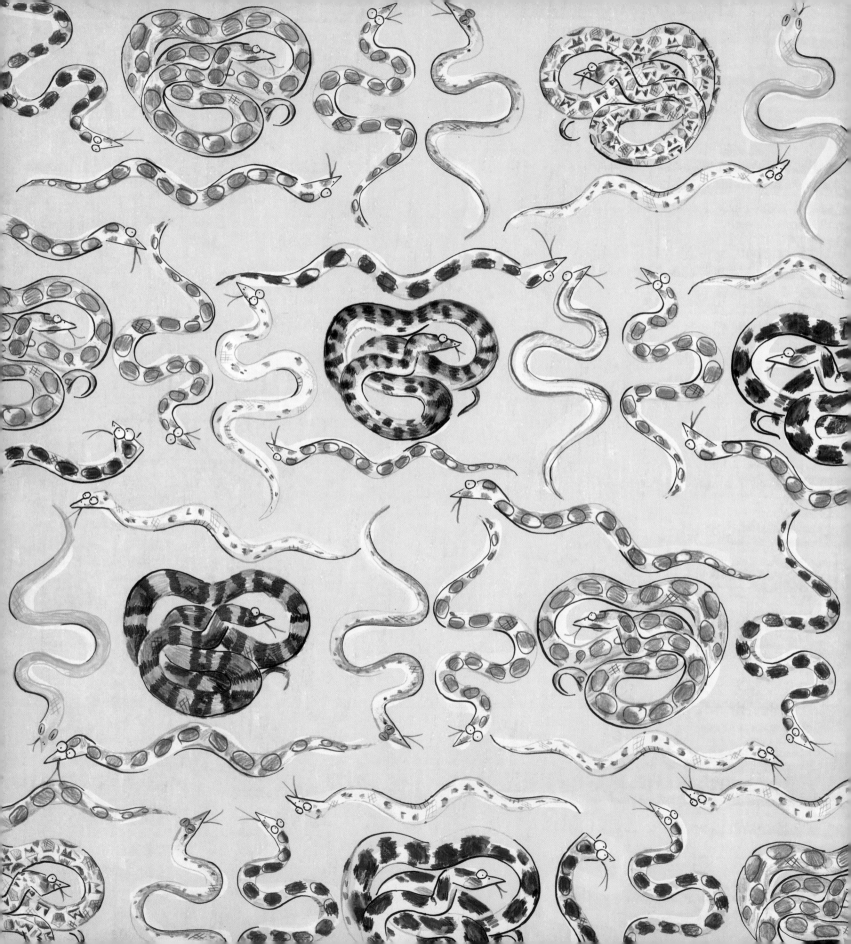

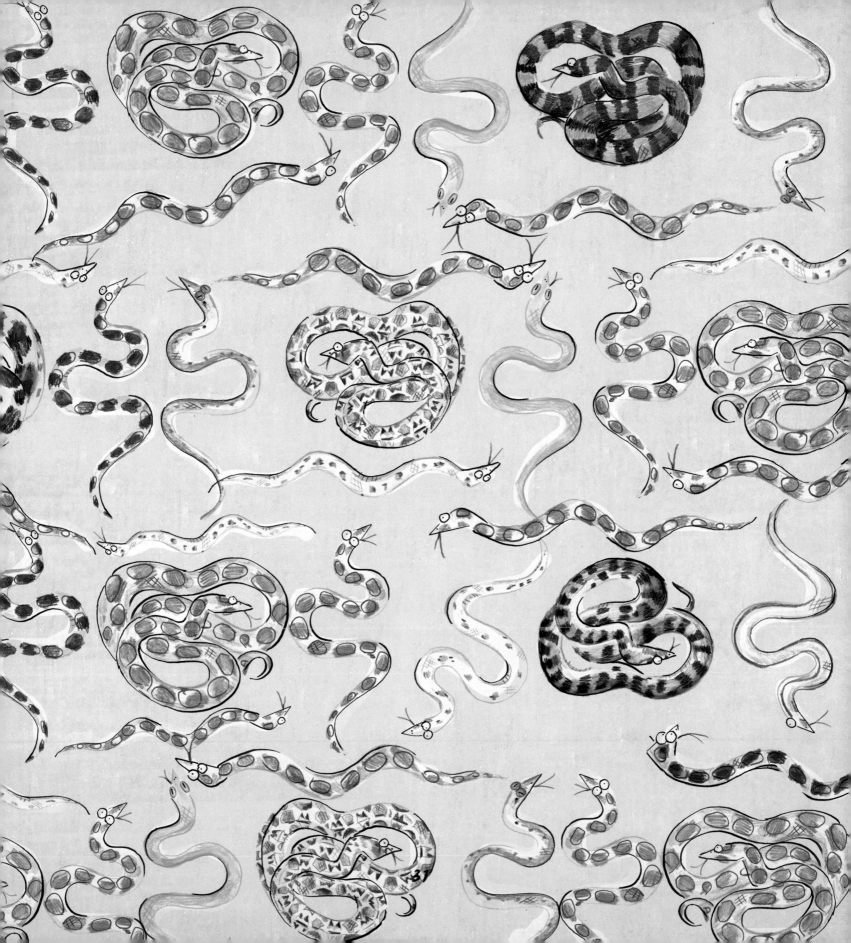

# Note to Parents

Sharing books with children is one of the best ways to help them learn. And it's one of the best ways they learn to read, too.

Nature Storybooks are beautifully illustrated, award-winning information picture books whose focus on animals has a strong appeal for children. They can be read as stories, revisited and enjoyed again and again, inviting children to become excited about a subject, to think and discover, and to want to find out more.

Each book is an adventure into the real world that broadens children's experience and develops their curiosity and understanding – and that's the best kind of learning there is.

# Note to Teachers

Nature Storybooks provide memorable reading experiences for children in Key Stages 1 and 2 (Years 1–4), and also offer many learning opportunities for exploring a topic through words and pictures.

By working with the stories, either individually or together, children can respond to the animal world through a variety of activities, including drawing and painting, role play, talking and writing.

The books provide a rich starting-point for further research and for developing children's knowledge of information genres.

**Nature Storybooks support the literacy curriculum in a variety of ways, providing:**

- a focus for a whole class topic
- high-quality texts for guided reading
- a resource for the class read-aloud programme
- information texts for the class and school library for developing children's individual reading interests

Find more information on how to use Nature Storybooks in the classroom at
**www.walker.co.uk/naturestorybooks**

Nature Storybooks support KS 1–2 English and KS 1–2 Science